GROOVY

Matthew 6:26-34
—J.D.

For my wonderful children, Trey & Destiny;
your talents and gifts inspire me! Mom
1 Peter 4:10
—K.D.

Pete the Cat and the New Guy

Text copyright © 2014 by Kimberly and James Dean

All rights reserved. Printed in the United states of America.

No part of this book may be used or reproduced in any manner whatsoever without

written permission except in the case of brief quotations embodied in critical articles and reviews.

For information address HarperCollins Children's Books, a division of HarperCollins Publishers,

10 East 53rd Street, New York, NY 10022.

www.harpercollinschildrens.com

Library of Congress Cataloging-in-Publication Data

Dean, Kim, date.

Pete the Cat and the new guy / Kimberly and James Dean. — First edition.

pages   cm

Summary: Pete the Cat and his animal friends welcome Gus the Platypus, who discovers his own

special talent.

ISBN 978-0-06-227560-8 (hardcover)

ISBN 978-0-06-227561-5 (library)

[1. Stories in rhyme. 2. Cats—Fiction. 3. Platypus—Fiction. 4. Animals—Fiction. 5. Friendship—

Fiction. 6. Individuality—Fiction.] I. Dean, James, date. II. Title.

PZ8.3.D3443Pe 2014   2013047955

[E]—dc23   CIP

                                                                                          AC

The artist used pen and ink, with watercolor and acrylic paint, on

300lb hot press paper to create the illustrations for this book.

Typography by Jeanne L. Hogle

14 15 16 17 18   LP   10 9 8 7 6 5 4 3 2 1

❖

First Edition

Pete the Cat

and the New Guy

MOOHAUL MOOVERS

MOVING BOX

HANDLE WITH CARE

Kimberly and James Dean

HARPER

An Imprint of HarperCollinsPublishers

It was Sunday, and Pete's friends had come to play!
They were rocking to a new song when . . .

BEEP BEEP BEEP

There was a noise coming from across the street!

Wise Old Owl had a view from his tree.
Pete said, "Hey, Owl! What do you see?"
Owl said, "All I see are green shoes and a red hat."
Pete answered, "Sounds like my kind of cat!"

Pete could not imagine who this new guy could be.
"I really hope it's a new friend for me."

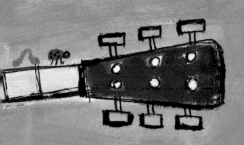

On Monday . . .
Pete wanted to say hi, but
he was feeling kind of shy,

so he just rode by and
by and by and by—

until finally Pete got to meet the new guy.

Pete said, "I've never met anyone quite like you!
You seem like a duck, and like a beaver too!"
The new guy said to Pete, "Hi, my name is Gus.
Glad to meet you. I'm a platypus."

Pete said, "You're not like me, and I am not like you, but I think being different is really very cool."

On Tuesday . . .
Pete and Gus took a walk down the street.
They came to Squirrel, who was playing in a tree.

"Hi, Gus," said Squirrel. "Climbing is easy. Try and see."

Gus gave the tree a try, but the branch
was way too high.
"I wish I could climb like you, but climbing
is something I just can't do."

Pete said,
"Don't be sad,
don't be blue.
There is something
everyone can do!"

On Wednesday . . .
Pete and Gus took a walk down the street.
They came to Pete's friend Grumpy Toad, who said, "Come play leapfrog with me! Jumping is easy. Try and see."

Gus jumped and leaped, but he couldn't get over Toad or Pete.

"I wish I could jump like you, but jumping is something I just can't do."

Pete said,
"Don't be sad,
don't be blue.
There is something
everyone can do!"

On Thursday . . .
Pete and Gus took a walk down the street.
Soon they saw Octopus, who said, "Come juggle with me! Juggling is easy! Try and see!"

"I wish I could juggle like you, but juggling is something I just can't do."

Pete said,
"Don't be sad,
don't be blue.
There is something
everyone can do!"

On Friday . . .
Pete and Gus took a walk down the street.
Gus said, "I can't juggle or jump or climb a tree.
It's no fun around here for me."

On Saturday . . .
Pete hoped Gus would come out to play.

"I wish Gus wasn't sad—
I wish Gus wasn't blue—
I wish there was something
we could do."

Just then Pete heard a groovy sound.
It was coming from across the street.
Gus was rocking to his own beat.

SWEET!

Pete said,
"Check out Gus the Platypus.
He found something cool he
can do with us!"

= =
TAP
=

THUMP
THUMP